145658 EN
Midget Cars

Niver, Heather Moore
ATOS BL 4.4
Points: 0.5

FAST Lane
OPEN-WHEEL RACING

MIDGET CARS

By Heather Moore Niver

Gareth Stevens
Publishing

Please visit our website, www.garethstevens.com. For a free color catalog of all our high-quality books, call toll free 1-800-542-2595 or fax 1-877-542-2596.

Library of Congress Cataloging-in-Publication Data

Niver, Heather Moore.
Midget cars / Heather Moore Niver.
     p. cm. — (Fast lane: open-wheel racing)
Includes index.
ISBN 978-1-4339-5764-2 (pbk.)
ISBN 978-1-4339-5765-9 (6-pack)
ISBN 978-1-4339-5762-8 (library binding)
1. Midget cars (Automobiles) I. Title.
TL236.6.N48 2012
629.222—dc22

                              2011006074

First Edition

Published in 2012 by
Gareth Stevens Publishing
111 East 14th Street, Suite 349
New York, NY 10003

Copyright © 2012 Gareth Stevens Publishing

Designer: Daniel Hosek
Editor: Greg Roza

Photo credits: Cover, pp. 1, 9 (Bobby Santos III), 15 Shutterstock.com; pp. 4–5, 6–7 (all images), 9 (main image), 12–13, 17 courtesy Jeff Arns; p. 11 Harry Todd/Hulton Archive/Getty Images; p. 13 (Kevin Swindell) Rusty Jarrett/Getty Images; pp. 18–19 Racing One/ISC Archives/Getty Images.

Printed in the United States of America

CPSIA compliance information: Batch #CS11GS: For further information contact Gareth Stevens, New York, New York at 1-800-542-2595.

CONTENTS

Words in the glossary appear in **bold** type the first time they are used in the text.

START YOUR ENGINES!

Auto racing is a contest between two or more motor vehicles. The vehicles commonly race around a track. The winner is the first driver to cross the finish line. There are many exciting kinds of auto racing. Midget car racing is one of them.

Midget cars are small and light, but they have powerful engines. This makes them fast! Midget car races take place all over the United States. They're also very popular in Australia and New Zealand.

Driver Levi Jones leads Steve Buckwalter into a turn on a dirt track.

WHAT'S A MIDGET CAR?

The midget car's **chassis** is made from the kind of steel used to make airplanes. Midget cars have an open **cockpit** and an upright seat for the driver.

To enter a United States Auto Club (USAC) midget car race, a midget car must weigh at least 900 pounds (408 kg), not including the driver. The **wheelbase** must be between 66 and 76 inches (168 and 193 cm). The cars can't be more than 65 inches (165 cm) wide. Most are 10 feet (3 m) long.

Fast Fact

Sprint cars are another type of small race car. They're larger than midgets. They're smaller than full-size race cars, but they have the same power.

sprint car

Brad Loyet became the Midget Car Rookie of the Year in 2005 when he was just 18 years old.

THE MIGHTY MIDGET ENGINE

Don't let their small size fool you. Midget cars create some serious power! Most midget car engines can produce between 325 and 350 **horsepower** (HP). The power comes from engines with four or six **cylinders**. The most popular engine has four cylinders.

Midget car engines are **fuel** injected. This means that the fuel is sprayed through small jets and then ignited, or lit on fire. Midget cars burn **methanol** and can hold at least 28 gallons (106 l).

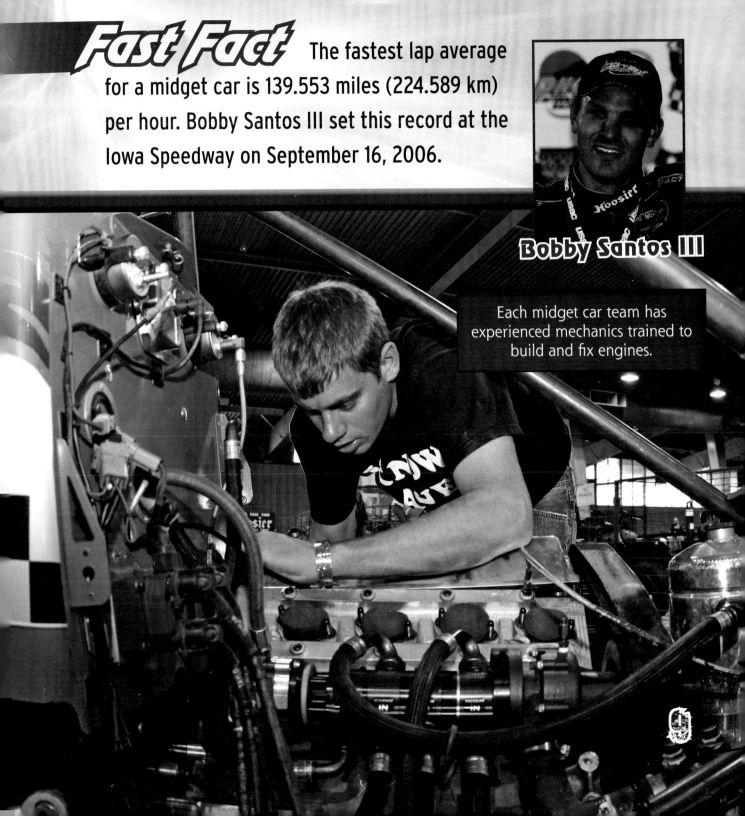

Bobby Santos III

Each midget car team has experienced mechanics trained to build and fix engines.

STARTING SIMPLE

Midget cars, or "doodlebugs," were born in 1919. Some kids in Los Angeles, California, built them to race in the Junior College Stadium.

Midget car racing officially became a sport on August 10, 1933. Times were hard, and not everyone could afford to race and fix full-size cars. Builders removed unnecessary parts from their cars to make them lighter and cheaper to fix. They used engines from old cars, motorcycles, and even airplanes! By the 1950s, you could build a tiny "micro midget" for only $300.

Early midget cars—like this one driven by British champion Jean Reville—were even smaller and simpler than today's cars.

Fast Fact The name "midget" was also used for a tiny car made for ordinary driving that appeared in the 1940s. The King Midget was sold as a kit or a completed car.

Midget cars can zoom up to speeds greater than 150 miles (241 km) per hour. Races can be from 2.5 to 25 miles (4 to 40 km) long. There are local, regional, and even international races.

Midget car races are usually kept short for safety reasons. It can be unsafe to drive long distances in a small car with so much power. Crashes are common, and there can even be explosions! To help keep drivers safe, midget cars have **roll cages** and **roll bars.**

Fast Fact

In 2011, Kevin Swindell won a midget car race called the Chili Bowl. He also won this race in 2010.

Kevin Swindell

Midget cars are light and fast. Crashes and rollovers are common.

13

QUARTER MIDGETS

Quarter midget cars are even smaller than regular midget cars. As the name suggests, they're usually a quarter the size of a midget car. Their frame is tube shaped. Drivers can paint the body any way they want. Like regular midget cars, quarter midgets have roll cages and special seat belts.

Kids from 5 to 16 years old can race quarter midgets. The cars and rules are all planned for their safety. There are 50 quarter midget racing clubs across the country.

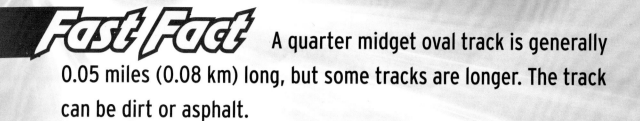

Everything on a quarter midget car—from the tires to the chassis—is smaller than a regular midget car.

WHO'S BEHIND THE WHEEL?

Midget cars might be smaller than full-size cars, but you don't have to be small to drive them. However, you do have to be a quick, smart driver.

Many of the world's greatest racers got their start in midget cars. NASCAR superstar Jeff Gordon was a national quarter-midget champion at age 8! The great driver A.J. Foyt won his first **professional** race in a midget car. He went on to become the first four-time winner of the Indianapolis 500!

Drivers Gavin Galbraith and Scott Hatton bump together as they battle for the lead.

A Formula Libre, or Free Formula, race lets drivers race any kind of car they want. On July 25, 1959, a Formula Libre race was held on an asphalt track at Lime Rock Park, Connecticut. Rodger Ward raced his midget car against expensive sports cars. His car was light, but powerful enough to beat all the full-size cars. Drivers and fans were shocked! Ward's win is so well known in some racing circles that it's sometimes simply called "*the* race."

Some midget car racers are daredevils on the track. They even have names like "Daring" Bill Zaring.

Rodger Ward's front tire comes up off the track during a race in the early 1960s.

19

MIDGET CAR MOVIES

Midget cars were so popular in the first half of the 1900s that they got lots of screen time. In the 1950 movie *To Please a Lady* (also called *Red Hot Wheels*), actor Clark Gable played a wild midget car driver who was banned from the tracks. Lots of the movie's racing scenes were filmed at the Indianapolis Motor Speedway. The movie featured real-life drivers, too. Other midget car movies include *Ten Laps to Go*, *Speed to Spare*, and *The Big Wheel*.

MIDGET CAR NUMBERS

Weight	at least 900 pounds (408 kg) without driver
Chassis	aircraft steel
Horsepower	325 to 350 HP
Engine	no more than six cylinders (usually four)
Fuel	methanol, at least 28 gallons (106 l)
Wheelbase	66 to 76 inches (168 to 193 cm)
Width	at most 65 inches (165 cm)
Length	about 10 feet (3 m)

GLOSSARY

asphalt: a natural matter used to make roads

chassis: steel tubes put together to carry the engine, seats, and other parts of a car

cockpit: the place where the driver sits

cylinder: a tube-shaped space in an engine in which a part called a piston moves up and down to create power

fuel: something that is burned to create power

horsepower: the measure of the power produced by an engine

methanol: a powerful fuel used in rockets and dragsters

professional: having to do with a job someone does for a living

roll bar: a padded metal bar on a car that helps keep the driver safe in case the car rolls over

roll cage: a framework of metal bars around the driver

wheelbase: the distance between the centers of the front and back wheels

Books

Maddox, Jake. *Speedway Switch*. Minneapolis, MN: Stone Arch Books, 2007.

O'Leary, Mike. *Rodger Ward: Superstar of American Racing's Golden Age*. St. Paul, MN: Motorbooks, 2006.

Websites

National Midget Auto Racing Hall of Fame

www.worthyofhonor.com
Read about today's midget car drivers, hall of fame members, and races.

QuarterMidgets.com

www.quartermidgets.com
Check out quarter midget racing schedules, news, and activities.

United States Auto Club

www.usacracing.com
Read all about the latest in midget car races and race schedules, and view photos and video of races.

INDEX